To Sean,
our moms & dads
and Mr. Yellow in the sky

SEAN AWESOME

A Mission at Night

By Ms. Yellow and Mr. Wide

This is **Sean Awesome**.

Before he was born, his Mommy and Daddy
wanted to be awesome for each other.

So they changed their last name to Awesome.
That's how Sean became Sean Awesome.

In general, Sean's life WAS awesome,
until one night...

"Sean Awesome! You are a big boy now. You
have to start sleeping in your own room," said
Mommy. But Sean didn't want to sleep in his
own room. He was scared to sleep all by himself.

So, tucked under his blanket, Sean thought and thought about how to sneak into Mommy's room without her noticing. Sean waited for the perfect moment to start his mission.

Quietly, he got up and went into the kitchen. He grabbed a giant black tablecloth from the cabinet. He put it over his head. Now he was invisible.

He walked very carefully all the way to Mommy's room. But he couldn't see anything through the black cloth.

BANG!

He walked right into the door.

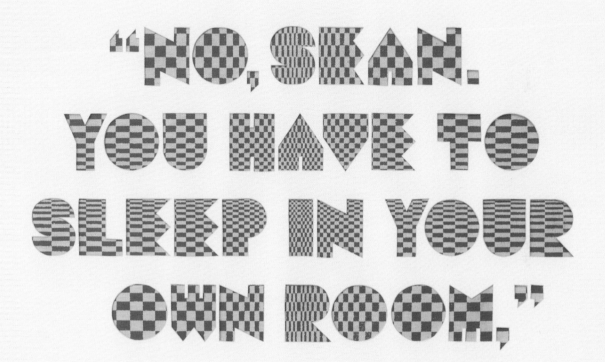

"NO, SEAN. YOU HAVE TO SLEEP IN YOUR OWN ROOM,"

said Mommy.

Mission failed.

But Sean didn't give up. He had a new idea.

Sean put on his Halloween costume.

He slithered on his tummy all the way to Mommy's room.

He managed to stand up, but it was very hard to open the door without any hands.

So he tried to turn the knob with his chin.

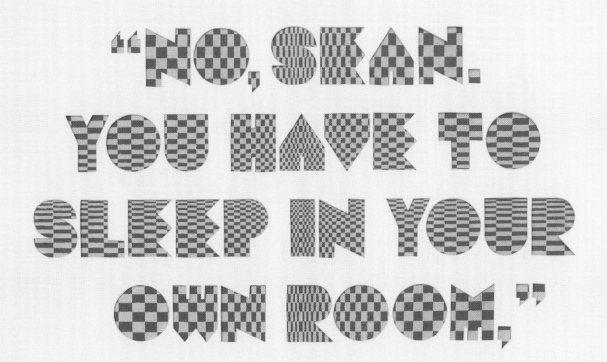

"NO, SEAN.
YOU HAVE TO
SLEEP IN YOUR
OWN ROOM,"

said Mommy.

Mission failed.

Back in his room, Sean dug through his toy

chest and found a big black hat.

Aha!

Sean put on his black sunglasses and drew a mustache on his face.

He looked just like a secret agent,
perfect for sneaking.

He tiptoed all the way to

Mommy's room

and gently opened the door.

He snuck over to the bed, but Mommy was not there. Sean looked around the room nervously. Where was she?

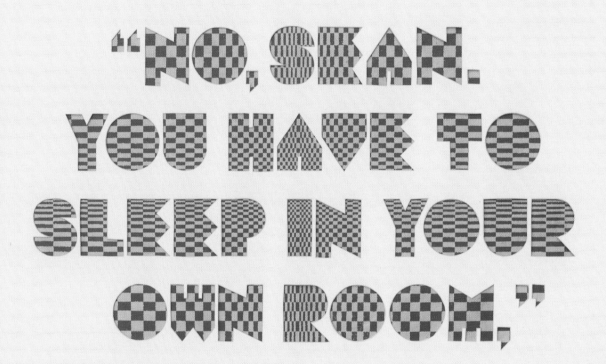

"NO, SEAN. YOU HAVE TO SLEEP IN YOUR OWN ROOM,"

said Mommy,

coming back from the bathroom.

Mission failed.

Then, Sean had the most awesome idea. He put on…

one radar wristband to check if Mommy was asleep,

one golden belt to light up the darkness,

one blue cape to fly quietly through the hallway,

and finally one red mask to make him brave.

First, he peeked out into the hallway.

Check!

Then, he slowly floated all the way to Mommy's room and opened the door.

Check!

Next, he swooped over to Mommy's bed.

Mommy was asleep.

Check!

Finally, he lifted the blanket and slid into bed.

Check!

"NO, S

YOU M

SLEEP

OWN

EAN.

VE TO

N YOUR

ROOM,"

said Mommy.

But the sun was shining through the window.

"Good morning!" said Sean with a big smile.

He had slept all night in Mommy's room.

Mission completed.

Sean was very proud of himself. He felt as if he could do anything.

That night, Sean looked through his closet and put on an astronaut suit. But this time, it was not for sneaking into Mommy's room.
It was for a new mission in his own room.

5, 4, 3, 2, 1...

Sean blasted off into his dreams.

Mission accomplished.

The End

Some time before Sean was born...

When Sky (Daddy) proposed to Ginger (Mommy), he promised to be an awesome husband. In return Ginger promised to be an awesome wife. Later they came up with the idea of being Awesome in name too.

Ginger and Sky became a real Awesome family with the birth of their child, Sean Awesome.

Published in 2018 by Simply Read Books
www.simplyreadbooks.com
Text © 2018 Jiwon Hwang
Illustrations © 2018 Sung Hong

Library and Archives Canada Cataloguing in Publication
Hwang, Jiwon, author Sean Awesome : a mission at night / written by Jiwon
Hwang ; illustrated by Sung Hong.

ISBN 978-1-77229-029-5 (hardcover)

I. Hong, Sung, illustrator   II. Title.
PS8615.W36S43 2018   jC813´.6   C2018-900296-4

We gratefully acknowledge for their financial support of our publishing
program the Canada Council for the Arts, the BC Arts Council, and the
Government of Canada.

Manufactured in Malaysia
Book design by Naomi MacDougall

10 9 8 7 6 5 4 3 2 1